P9-DNK-523

NOV - 1996

DISCARD

ORLAND PARK PUBLIC LIBRARY
AILEEN S. ANDREW MEMORIAL
14760 PARK LANE
ORLAND PARK, ILLINOIS 60462
349-8138

DEMCO

Roly-Poly Puppies

A Counting Book

ORLAND PARK PUBLIC LIBRARY

Roly-Poly Puppies

A Counting Book

by Elaine Moore • Illustrated by Jacqueline Rogers

SCHOLASTIC INC.

New York Toronto London Auckland Sydney

ORLAND PARK PUBLIC LIBRARY

For Wendy, Tuli, Sugar, Sassy, Yogi,
Hershey, Jesse, Maxi, Cleo, and Boots
—E.M.

To B.I.T.S. Farm
—J.R.

Text copyright © 1996 by Elaine Moore.
Illustrations copyright © 1996 by Jacqueline Rogers.
All rights reserved. Published by Scholastic Inc.
CARTWHEEL BOOKS and the CARTWHEEL BOOKS logo are registered trademarks of Scholastic Inc.

No part of this publication may be reproduced in whole or in part, or stored in a retrieval system,
or transmitted in any form or by any means, electronic, mechanical, photocopying, recording, or otherwise,
without written permission of the publisher. For information regarding permission,
write to Scholastic Inc., 555 Broadway, New York, NY 10012.

Library of Congress Cataloging-in-Publication Data

Moore, Elaine.
 Roly-poly puppies : a counting book / by Elaine Moore;
illustrated by Jacqueline Rogers.
 p.   cm. — (Story corner)
 Summary: Rhyming text and illustrations introduce numbers one through ten
as an ever-growing group of puppies plays outdoors.
 ISBN 0-590-46665-8
 [1. Counting.   2. Dogs—Fiction.   3. Stories in rhyme.]
 I. Rogers, Jacqueline, ill.   II. Title.   III. Series.
 PZ8.3.M7832Ro   1996
 [E]—dc20   95-30067
                                                                      CIP
                                                                      AC

12 11 10 9 8 7 6 5 4 3 2 1   6 7 8 9 0/09

Printed in Singapore   10

First Scholastic printing, September 1996

1 roly-poly puppy
sleeps in the hay.

Here comes another puppy.

He wants to play.

2 roly-poly puppies
run around a tree.
Here comes another puppy.

Now there are **3**.
Three roly-poly puppies
play tug-of-war.
Here comes another puppy.

Now there are **4**.
Four roly-poly puppies
sniff at a hive.
Here comes another puppy.

Now there are **5**.
Five roly-poly puppies
are doing puppy tricks.
Here comes another puppy.

Now there are **6**.
Six roly-poly puppies
eat at eleven.
Here comes another puppy.

Now there are **7**.

Seven roly-poly puppies
tumble out the gate.
Whoops! There's another puppy.

ORLAND PARK PUBLIC LIBRARY

Now there are **8**.

Eight roly-poly puppies
trot in a line.
Here comes another puppy.

Now there are **9**.
Nine roly-poly puppies
come home to their pen.
Is there another puppy?

Yes, there are **10**.

Ten roly-poly puppies
drop in a heap.
Ten tired puppies
fall fast asleep.

ORLAND PARK PUBLIC LIBRARY